One day, an old woman came to the door selling trinkets. "These were made in London – where everyone's rich and the streets are paved with gold!" she told Dick.

"Surely I'll change my luck and make my fortune if I go there!" Dick thought to himself.

He decided to leave for London at once.

Dick took all the food he had in his house – half a stale loaf of bread, a corner of cheese and a wrinkled apple.

Then he set off. He could picture the golden streets of London glowing in the sun.

4

Dick
Whittington

Retold by Kate Scott

Illustrated by Ruth Hammond

Collins

Dick Whittington lived in a cold, damp cottage at the end of a long, muddy track. Each morning, his boots sank into the mud as he fetched water from the well. Each day, he worked in the fields until his body ached. Each night, he tried to warm himself in front of his fire.

"How I wish I could change my luck," Dick said to himself.

Dick walked along the hard, dusty roads until the sun dropped down behind the hills. He lay under a tree and listened to the wind whispering in the leaves overhead.

"Your luck will change," the wind seemed to say as he fell asleep. "You'll find your fortune."

Dick woke up cold and aching, but the thought of London made him leap up from the hard ground. He ran to the stream to wash. The water was icy cold but Dick didn't care – he was too excited about what he might find in London.

When he saw London appear ahead of him, Dick couldn't wait to see the streets of gold. He began to run. Any moment now, he'd see the city where his luck would change.

But London didn't look very much like Dick had imagined it. London didn't look *anything* like Dick had imagined it. The streets weren't paved with gold. They were just ordinary, cold, grey cobbles like everywhere else. And there were so many people! People were pushing and shoving and shouting everywhere he looked.

8

"How'll I find my luck and fortune here?" Dick thought.

He sat down on an empty wooden box and put his head in his hands. He was tired and hungry and he'd nowhere to go.

"That's a long face," said a kind voice.

Dick looked up. In front of him was a tall man in velvet robes embroidered with gold thread.

The merchant smiled. "Did you come to London to find your fortune?"

Dick nodded. "And to change my luck," he said miserably.

The man patted him on the back. "Well, perhaps you have changed your luck. I'm looking for someone to work in my house. Would you like a job? And maybe a hot meal, too?"

Dick jumped to his feet. "Yes please!"

"Excellent! Follow me!" said the merchant, and he led the way. They walked through the crowds that were jostling and chattering around them. Every now and then, the merchant turned to give Dick an encouraging smile.

Dick hoped that everyone at the merchant's house would be as kind as the merchant. But they weren't …

The merchant's home was a grand building of grey stone. Inside, there were so many rooms Dick thought five families could've lived in it!

The merchant took Dick down to a large kitchen where the cook was busy preparing that night's dinner.

"Here we are," the merchant told the cook cheerfully. "I've brought Dick to help you with your work!"

"Very kind of you, sir, thank you," said the cook. But Dick saw that the cook didn't look at all happy with the news.

As soon as the merchant was gone, the cook scowled. "I wanted someone strong to work for me, not a scrawny lad like you."

The cook put Dick to work washing up every pot and pan in the house. They were covered in crusts of food and smelt like old socks, sour milk and fish.

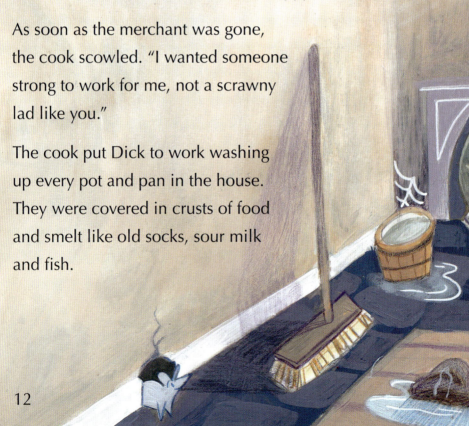

Afterwards, Dick had to peel the potatoes, chop the cabbage and stir the vast vat of soup until his arm ached. Then there was more washing up! Dick tried his best but the cook never seemed to be happy with him.

"Can't you go any faster?" the cook shouted.

"I'm sorry," Dick said. He tried to speed up, but the cook still scowled.

13

When Dick was finally allowed to go to his room, he was so tired that he was sure he'd fall asleep right away.

But that was before he found out about the rats …

As Dick lay down on his narrow, lumpy bed, he heard scratching – and scrabbling – and scuffling. He lit his candle and saw rats everywhere! There were rats under the bed, beside the bed, and up on the windowsill.

"I must be the most unlucky boy in the world!" Dick thought, his eyes filling with tears.

He decided he had to leave. He'd find another job – and a room with no rats!

The streets were cold and dark. Dick walked along with his arms wrapped around himself, shivering in his thin shirt.

The church bells rang out and Dick stood for a moment to listen. As the delicate chime of the bells sounded, Dick heard a voice carried on the wind: "Turn again, Whittington, three times Lord Mayor of London."

The voice repeated, "Turn again, Whittington, three times Lord Mayor of London."

"That can't be a message for me," Dick said to himself and carried on walking.

But again the voice repeated. "Turn again, Whittington, three times Lord Mayor of London."

Dick stopped. "The voice must mean me! Perhaps my luck's going to change at last."

Dick decided to do as the bells had told him and he turned back towards the merchant's house. As he neared the merchant's door, a cat ran out from the shadows. The cat purred loudly, then looked up at Dick and meowed.

Dick bent down and stroked the cat for a moment and then walked on. The cat followed Dick and meowed again. Dick was struck by a thought. "Will you keep the rats away?" he asked the cat. The cat purred more loudly than ever.

Dick lay down in his bed with the cat beside him. The rats scurried away as soon as they saw the sharp claws of the cat, and the cat's loud purrs made Dick feel he wasn't alone.

The next day, as Dick was carrying a pile of plates, a young girl poked her head out of a door. Dick's cat ran straight up to her and began weaving in and out of her legs.

"Hello!" said the girl. "Is that your cat?"

"Yes," Dick said.

The girl's name was Alice. She was the merchant's daughter.

"I've no one to talk to because my father's away so often," she told Dick.

Dick laughed. "And I've no one to talk to – except my cat! Maybe we could be friends?"

Alice smiled. "I'd like that."

One afternoon, the merchant gathered all the servants in the dining hall. "I'm going on a voyage to trade some goods with a rich king. If you've anything of value, you can give it to me and I'll bring you back what I receive for it."

There was a buzz of excitement as the servants went to find what they could give the merchant. But what could Dick possibly have to sell?

Dick's cat purred loudly and wound himself tightly around Dick's legs.

Dick picked up his cat and held him close. "Will you be my fortune?"

The cat purred more loudly than ever. So Dick brought the cat to the merchant.

The merchant laughed. "A cat? I've never traded anything like this before!"

"Please," said Dick. "I think he could bring me my fortune."

"I hope he does," the merchant said kindly. He took the cat and promised to bring back whatever he got for him.

The next day, the merchant set off on his voyage, on a ship laden with precious goods and, of course, Dick's cat.

Dick missed his cat, but every day he became better friends with Alice. They looked at the globe and talked about the places Alice's father and Dick's cat might be.

"Wherever my cat is," Dick said, "I know he'll be scaring rats!"

At last, the merchant returned and called for Dick to come and see him. The merchant smiled. "You were right about that cat, Dick."

Dick grinned. "You sold my cat?"

The merchant laughed. "Indeed I did! For more gold than I've ever seen! You're richer than I am!"

Dick's mouth gaped. "I'm – rich?"

The merchant told Dick how the royal court of the king had been plagued with rats. "And then your cat came along," said the merchant. "He scared off every last rat – and so, became more precious to the king than anything else on my ship."

"Your cat did bring you luck and change your fortune," Alice told Dick.

Dick smiled. "But, best of all, he brought me good friends," he said.

After that, Dick lived in the merchant's house but no longer worked for the cook. He and Alice still looked at the globe in the garden but now they planned the journeys they'd take when they were older.

"One day, perhaps we can go and visit my cat," Dick said to Alice.

Alice smiled. "We can go everywhere!" she said.

And many years later, when Dick was grown, he became Mayor of London – three times, just as the bells had told him.

And far away, Dick's cat grew fat in the king's court. He purred so loudly it was a wonder Dick didn't hear him in London …

29

Dick's diary

15th July

If Alice wasn't here, I think I'd run away again.
The cook shouts at me every day and I miss
the sound of my cat purring in my room.
One good thing is that the rats have kept away
– my cat must've scared them off for good!

I wonder where the merchant's ship is now and
if my cat minds being at sea. Alice says one day
we could visit all the places her father's been.
I smile but I can't imagine it. She's very kind to
me and never shouts like the cook. She treats me
like a real friend, not a servant.

Becoming friends with her was all down to
my cat. I think even if the merchant doesn't sell
him, my cat's already brought me a fortune –
my friendship with Alice.

Dick

Ideas for reading

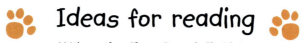

Written by Clare Dowdall, PhD
Lecturer and Primary Literacy Consultant

Reading objectives:
- increase familiarity with a wide range of books including fairy stories and retell orally
- discuss words and phrases that capture the reader's interest and imagination
- make predictions from details stated and applied
- identify main ideas drawn from more than one paragraph and summarise ideas

Spoken language objectives:
- participate in discussions, presentations, performances, role play, improvisations and debates

Curriculum links: PSHE – health and wellbeing: risk and resilience

Resources: ICT for research and making a portfolio; art materials

Build a context for reading
- Show the cover and ask children to share anything that they know about this famous traditional tale.
- Read the blurb. Ask children to try to describe London. Discuss whether the streets there are really paved with gold, and what this phrase might mean.
- Discuss whether the children would leave their homes to make their fortune when they're older. Think about the risks and the opportunities that might be involved.

Understand and apply reading strategies
- Read pp2–3 to the children. Discuss what they think about Dick and make a list of words to describe his character.
- Talk about what the phrase "make my fortune" means, and how Dick might make his fortune in London.